Choong. Choong. Choong. Choong.

A train slows to a stop at a station.

A conductor calls . . .

ALL ABOARD!

by **Mary Lyn Ray**

Illustrated by **Amiko Hirao**

Little, Brown and Company
BOSTON   NEW YORK   LONDON

And a rabbit gets on.
His name is Mr. Barnes.

Whoonk whoonk wahooonk. The train starts slow.

But then it begins to roll.

Long train, silver train. Long train, silver train.

Long train. Long train. Silver train. Silver train.
Train, train, train, train.

Whooo whoooooo

Red moons flash in the windows.

The train has left the city. Light has left the day.

Mr. Barnes yawns a small yawn.

In the coach cars, passengers
go to sleep in their seats.

In the sleepers, they do what Mr. Barnes does. He puts on his pajamas, he brushes his teeth in a little round sink, then he climbs in a bed that folds out of the wall and sleeps.

In the baggage car, boxes sleep.

Farms sleep, towns sleep, and ducks in watery
grasses sleep.

But far ahead in the cab, the engineer is awake.

The train has somewhere to go.

A city slides by, strung with lights in the night, like a tug of dreams on a river.

Only the engineer sees.

And maybe someone who watches, awake, out a window.

Coach, coach, coach, coach, sleeper car, sleeper car, coach, coach, sleeper car.

Sleeping cars.

Waking cars.

Mr. Barnes stretches. He pulls on his sleeves and buttons his buttons. He snaps his bed back in the wall, making a plush red seat to sit on.

In the coach cars, people wake, ruffling papers, looking drowsily at morning out the windows.

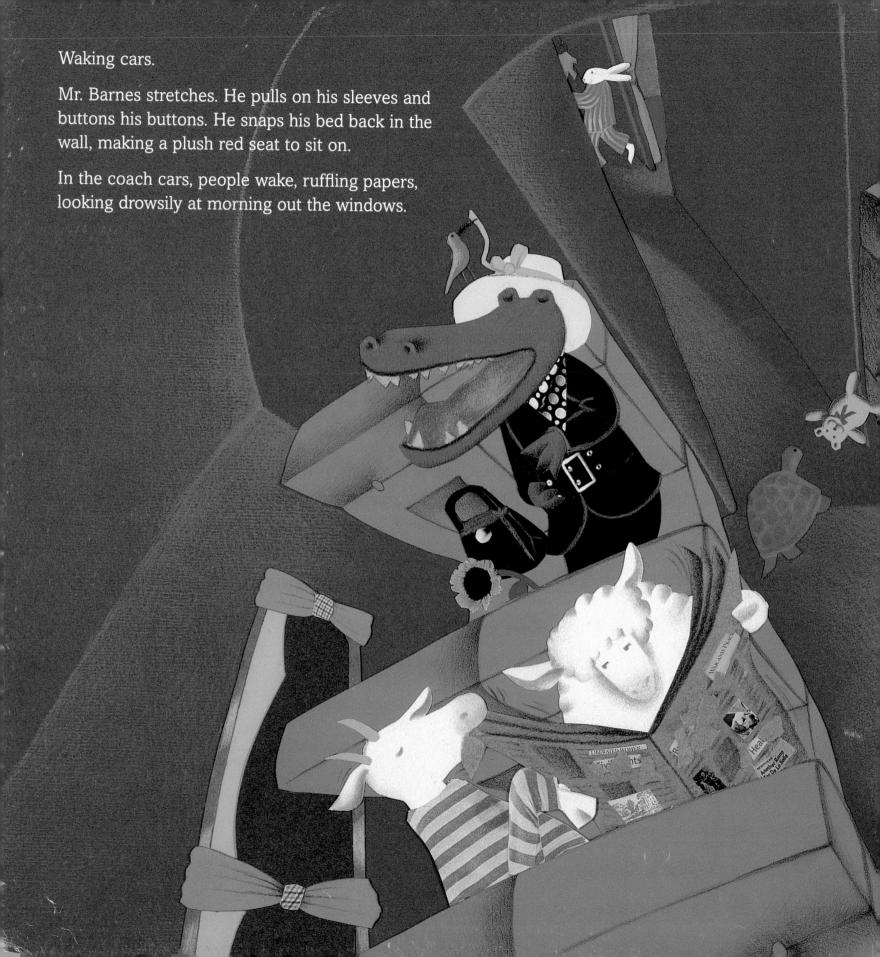

In the dining car, the chef begins to make breakfast.

Mr. Barnes shakes a white napkin over his lap and
orders a carrot muffin — because rabbits are supposed to eat
carrots — although it's hard to decline the French toast.

A freight flashes by.
Boxcar, coal car, tank car, flatcar.
Red red yellow green yellow yellow
blue green.
Vroom. Vroom. Vroom.
The freight has somewhere to go.

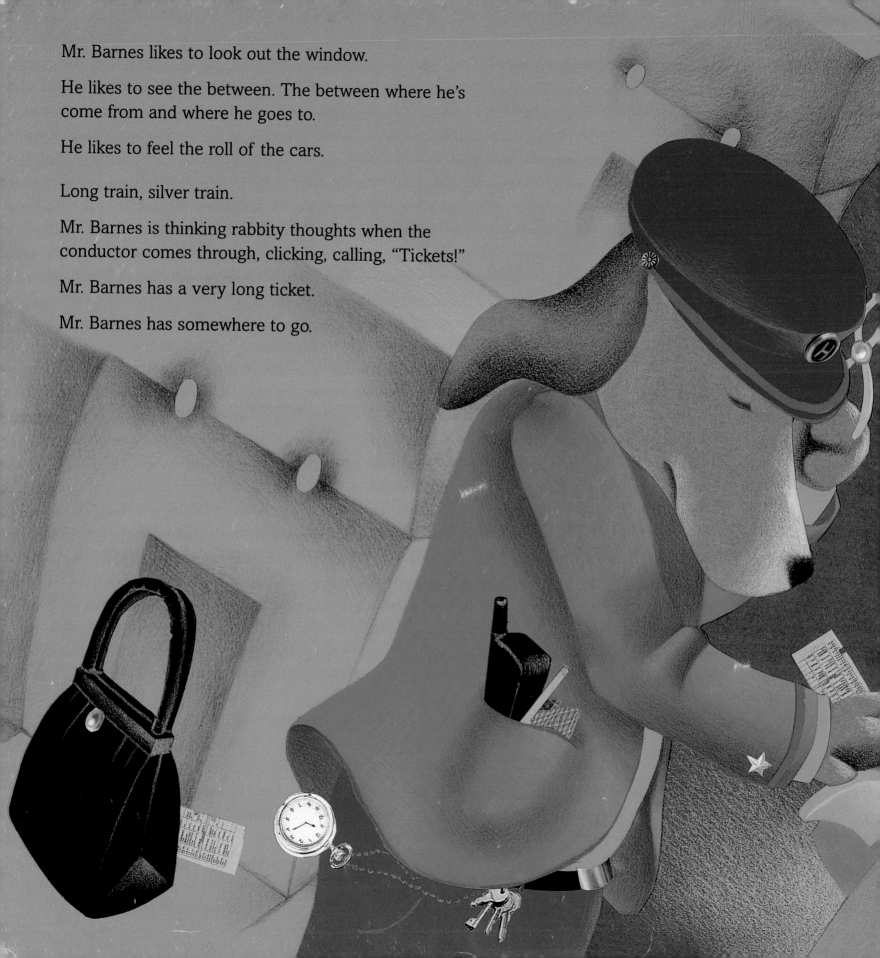

Mr. Barnes likes to look out the window.

He likes to see the between. The between where he's come from and where he goes to.

He likes to feel the roll of the cars.

Long train, silver train.

Mr. Barnes is thinking rabbity thoughts when the conductor comes through, clicking, calling, "Tickets!"

Mr. Barnes has a very long ticket.

Mr. Barnes has somewhere to go.

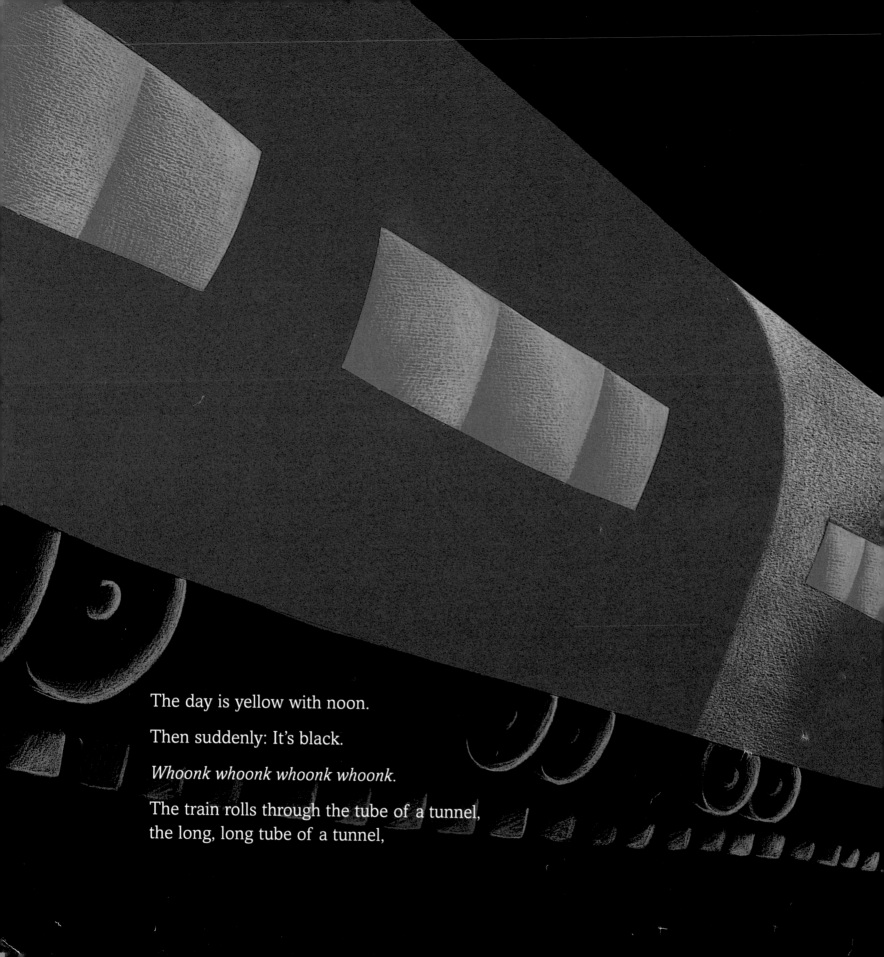

The day is yellow with noon.

Then suddenly: It's black.

Whoonk whoonk whoonk whoonk.

The train rolls through the tube of a tunnel,
the long, long tube of a tunnel,

back

into

sunlight.

Mr. Barnes waves at cars waiting at crossings.

Then his nose twitches. He smells the warm smells of lunch and returns to the dining car.

Again, he unfolds his napkin.

Plump after lunch, some passengers nap.

Some rummage for books and puzzles, some talk.

Some carry little cups from a fountain.

And some do what Mr. Barnes does. They sit at the window and look.

Up in the cab the engineer eats a sandwich.

Choong. Choong. Choong. Choong.

All day the train stops and starts and stops and starts.
Passengers get on, passengers get off.

But Mr. Barnes stays on the train.

Whooo whoooooo

It curls and whistles and rumbles and clacks
till somewhere —

it slows, it stops

and there Mr. Barnes gets off.

Arms go around him. Again, things go dark.
Mr. Barnes is mashed in a hug.

"Gramma, Grampa!"

The arms pull back.

Mr. Barnes has arrived.

But the train — "Allllll aboarrrrd!" — goes on.

Because the train still has somewhere to go.

Long train, silver train. Long train, silver train.

Long train. Long train. Silver train. Silver train.
Train, train, train, train.

Whooo whoooooo

For everyone who waves from trains,
and all those who wave back
—M.L.R.

For David and Ronnie,
with special thanks to Judy Sue
—A.H.

First Edition

Library of Congress Cataloging-in-Publication Data

Ray, Mary Lyn.
    All aboard! / by Mary Lyn Ray ; illustrated by Amiko Hirao. — 1st ed.
      p. cm.
    Summary: Mr. Barnes goes on a train trip and enjoys all the sights and sounds of the ride.
    ISBN 0-316-73507-8
    [1. Railroads—Trains—Fiction. 2. Rabbits—Fiction. 3. Toys—Fiction.]
I. Hirao, Amiko, ill. II. Title.

PZ7.R210154 Aj 2002
[E]—dc21   00-051464

10 9 8 7 6 5 4 3 2 1

NIL

Printed in Italy

The illustrations for this book were done in cut paper and colored pencil.
The text was set in Amasis, and the display type
is Maiandra Demi Bold.